WHAT DO YOU THINK?

Hey! I hope you are enjoying this book. Can you do me a small favor? Leave an honest review and let me know your thoughts, opinions, or criticism of this book. It takes less than 1 minute to leave a review and your reviews greatly help other readers find me work. Thank you so much!

Scan here!

Leave a review!

Made in the USA
Las Vegas, NV
05 January 2025

15917204R00057